The Book of Death

From the point of view of the Grimm Reaper

By

Edith Eaton

Dedication

For those who noticed, and stayed.
And to my cousin, Courtney Brown—thank you for
never letting go of my hand.

Epigraph

Some say death is the end.

Others say it's the beginning.

I say it's my job.

You don't have to like it—but you will meet me someday.

—The Grim Reaper

Preface

This isn't a grand book, and it's not trying to be. It's a small one — about quiet things, mostly. About endings, yes, but also about waiting. About being seen. About what lingers after we go.

I didn't set out to write about Death. He just showed up one day, same as he always does. Sat down like he had nowhere else to be. And then, so did she. The girl. I don't know where they came from exactly, but once they started talking, I kept listening.

Some of these pieces are stories. Some are just fragments — thoughts I couldn't let go of. There's truth in them, even if not all of it happened. Or maybe it did, just not in the way we usually measure.

If you've ever been curious about the one who comes at the end, or what it means to be marked, or what it feels like to be left behind — this is for you. And if not, that's all right too. We'll all understand eventually.

— Edith Eaton

Library of Congress

Cataloging-in-Publication Data

ISBN: 979-8-89397-506-2 (Paperback)

ISBN: 979-8-89397-507-9 (Hardcover)

Library of Congress Card Catalog Number

1-14918246151

Published by

Tolkeins Book Writing

Table of Contents

Prologue

Among the shadows I stand. I am part of one realm and part of another realm. Waiting for the sign to take what is mine.

I am death, the Grimm Reaper, but that's not all I do. It's just the only thing they, humans, remember me for. I just want one person to see the other side of me. I only take a soul when it has been marked.

I don't take just any soul I want; sometimes I wish I could, but there are laws that don't allow it. Even those that drive me crazy don't just get smacked. I have been at this job for millions of years. I hear them curse me and ask me why. I wish I could tell them why, but I can't…

At least that's what I thought, being unable to talk to humans, until I met a special girl. Not psychic or lying on her deathbed, special. Special because she could see me, and she wasn't marked. That part confused me.

Unknown to any of her friends and family, we would become friends ourselves. If not for her, I'd have lost myself in this task as my father and his father had done before me. If not for her, I'd be lost in this job as it drags me down.

We do this job for so long that we tend to forget the joy and wonders of the world. I was beginning to turn into that. Until I met her….

Chapter 1

The Mark

The mark appears solely on those nearing death. They don't see the mark; only the Reaper sees it.

If there is no mark, the person's time to die hasn't come yet. The only time anyone sees the Grimm Reaper is moments before they die. As he, the reaper, is about to reap the human soul for transit.

The mark isn't small, and an indicator light accompanies it. The mark gives the reaper an hour to reach the person. If he doesn't get them within the allocated time, the mark disappears, and they survive. When the mark fades, it might extend a life, even if only for a few minutes.

The reaper is punished for missing a mark, for each mark he misses. Some that manage to survive their first mark don't miss the second one. In some cases, the second time is years after the first one, for others it could be mere seconds or an hour away.

In all reality, why you're picked depends on where on his list your name falls. Yes, his list, God by all means is a man, but can, if needed can be a desired sex, race, or culture to fit in. He, the God, decides who dies, and who lives, not death, or Grimm Reaper. The reaper is, by all accounts, just the messenger, the transporter, and not more than that. Once the mark is given to you, only God can remove it. The only time he does so is if the reaper hasn't reached you within the time frame.

The mark is only seen by the reaper. The animal mark, followed by the guiding light, is either a black or red rose covered in thorns. Like the human reaper, the animal reaper can take the soul of the animals just before they die, and only if they have the mark.

The mark for humans isn't as nice. For humans, this mark is a skull wrapped in thorns with a bright red hash line. The red hash line glows a blood red and gets darker until either the reaper makes it to take the soul or misses the mark.

Since no other human can see this mark, passing it is instant. In fact, the passing of a human may take days. The mark just indicates that one will soon be passing. The mark of death itself isn't so grand. Most times it's a simple skull, sometimes it's the sheath of the reaper. The mark can never be removed. The only mark that can be removed is the indicator of death and the locator light once death has arrived.

Once a reaper reports into the marked person, the reaper or death mark is put upon them and can only be removed by death, in which the soul is reaped. This is where most of the waiting begins.

The finder's mark is given to someone by god under two pretenses. The first pretend is that his/her name is up on the list, and two that he/she managed to be skipped the first time around with the Reaper. Sometimes, on VERY rare occasions, God feels sympathy towards a marked one and for that He removes the mark.

He does sometimes allow a "miracle" to occur. Not that it's a "miracle" per se, but humans think it is, and to humor himself, God allows them to think a "miracle" has occurred. A "miracle" occurs sometimes because the reaper didn't make it on time or because god needs that human on earth a little longer.

When someone dies because of the given mark, many blame death, when it isn't at all responsible for what has occurred. All it is, the one to retrieve the soul.

The saying "don't shoot the messenger" applies to death. The messenger is just doing the job he is supposed to do. He will keep doing this job as long as God wants him to.

Something goes wrong. Humans call it an accident, but in our realm, we call it the sign. God has chosen you, and for us, it's a sign that we can see from anywhere in the world.

Everyone dies sooner or later. You will all die one day, and God would like to make your journey a little easier. That's where death comes in. God gives him the signal, which means your time is up.

Not everyone understands why they are taken, but those who do understand that one day it all ends are more willing to go with death. If you are marked, you won't know it…

The end, when death is seen standing by you, sheath in hand. His actions, so smooth and precise that you won't feel the pain when he makes his moves. If you are marked, but the reaper doesn't make it in time, you may be able to live a little longer. Just because you're saved doesn't mean you're safe. The mark can come back at any time.

The mark is meant only as an aid in locating the one that will soon be dying. The light gives the exact location like a GPS signal. Only death can see that. The color also indicates whether the animal or human reaper is to be intended.

For some, the thought of death is enough to frighten them. Therefore, the mark must be kept secret from all humans. It all comes down to the end of life.

Chapter 2

Death

I am there just before the silence, just before the others arrive. I come to carry your soul away. Take you to your next destination.

I am never seen, but always cursed out. I am always blamed for the unfinished business, and never thanked. I do what I am told, where my orders take me.

I have seen things many will never see. I have been blamed for things I have no control over. I do that of what I am told to do and only that of what I am told to do. When things go wrong, I am the one they blame first. It isn't my fault you fell off the stupid ladder; you know you should be watching what you are doing. All I am is His messenger. I do what He asks when He asks, and only that.

Ever since the day my father taught me everything I needed to know for this job, I've understood its importance. Now that I'm the only one left, his lessons matter more than ever. No matter how exhausted or worn down I am, I know I have to keep going with it, and I have no choice but to carry it out.

It has been a long time since I started this job. I arrive and leave only when I am ordered. I only take those He tells me to get, no more, no less. Well, sometimes less, if I miss the one I am supposed to go after. That's not entirely my fault, even though I am the one who gets chewed out for that. I know I have to be in many places at once, but sometimes being at all these places runs me down. I just can't seem to pull it together in time to make it, so every once in a while, one slips through. Then I am either on a mass collection pick up, or claiming the one I missed later in his/her life.

I know I am supposed to do exactly what He wants when He wants it, but sometimes I feel underappreciated and can't seem to get there on time. Oh well, there is always later. I know you're supposed to keep going, but it's hard when no one cares about you.

I deliver them to the transit station, pick up the next, and move on. I don't know any other job. I can't quit, what would happen then? I can imagine, and I don't like what I think.

So, until I am replaced, this is my job.

Here I'm not looking for sympathy. I don't give any, so I don't expect to get any. All I am trying to do is give you some understanding of 'why'.

It has to be done. The rules state one in and one out. For every child born, someone must die. The same rule applies to animals.

For instance, a baby is born, and a man dies in a shootout. The balance is sustained, so nothing goes wrong, but still, I need a rest sometimes. With how fast this human race populates, I am having issues keeping up….

Doctors claim people are living longer due to what they eat. I must protest, it is because I can't get there in the time I am allotted. So instead of dying, they live to be 100 plus, or die a few minutes later. When I finally get to them, those that reached 100 have no complaints.

Sometimes, I am even lucky to receive a thank you. Then at the transit station, "crossroads," I am lectured for taking so long to deliver this person. I can't keep up, and they won't slow down. The more they make, the more I have to take, but I can't sometimes…

As time goes on, I am to take even more… I often wonder if I just gave up, if anything would go wrong. Then I remember that the year Dad stopped, countries began to overcrowd. So, in order to reclaim the balance, He forced the hand to create havoc.

Sometimes, a massive storm is needed. Other times, it's an accident to get everything set back in order. For every year missed, a tragedy must strike to keep them aware that anything can happen.

It is not any easier, either taking one soul or 1,000 souls. The more you end up with, the more you have to manage. Let's face it, they never listen. That's why they end up dead in the first place.

The ones that make this job the hardest are the kids. Some haven't had a chance to be anything. Some never met their parents. But it's my job, and I have to do it, even if I don't want to.

Don't get me wrong, I'd rather let them all into this world, but I can't. I have a job, and I have to fulfil it. I do, though every so often, I don't seem joyful. The expression on a human's face when a "miracle" happens is a great feeling.

Sometimes the "miracle" happens just because I can't get there, but their joy… they are filled with relief, and I let it go. Once the mark is gone, I can't do anything anyway.

I don't mind letting a few get away, but there is no lingering upon it. I have more souls to get. More to take to the transit station, more to see off as they either start a new life or see the end.

I sometimes see the same people. Some are the same color or race as before. Even the same age, while some are so different, I don't recognize them. I know it's a way of life… or death, but sometimes I wish it didn't have to be done.

It does. This world can only handle so many at once. Without me, things might spiral out of control. So, until he decides I'm no longer needed, it's back to work. The longer I take to reach them, the more his frustration and anger grow.

At some places, I am as loved as an angel, but sadly, I am not. I am not a soul in any way, yet I must be. In order to feel, there has to be something inside me. Yet he tells me "no" and "get back to it." When I ask him, "What am I?" he simply says, "DEATH."

A five-letter word that has the power to change anyone, yet I have no soul. Just once, I'd like someone to be ok with what I have to do to them.

All the crying, screaming, cursing, and hitting are getting me a little down. I know they don't understand, and I wish I could tell them why, but I am not allowed to talk to them. Not even in their spirit form. I am only allowed to show them to the transit station.

From there, it is up to the travel agent. "Angle of direction" to send them to where they go next.

I can't even talk to Him, because I have too much to do. I see Him have conversations that last four hours or even days, and I feel sad. Just once, one time is all I ask, but He tells me no.

My dad said it happens. Just once, but we never let it go. That one that can see and hear us. Dad found his one, one million two hundred and seventeen years into it. Grandpa found his one, 100,000 years into it. So, I guess it could, but with all this work, I doubt it.

Mud slides, school shootings, man on a rampage on a base, and I am off. No time to dream, no time for myself. More in, more out, or am I trying to reset myself? Have I missed too many? I don't even know, but I can't waste time.

Chapter 3

The Dream

The first time I dreamed of her was about three weeks ago. I dreamed about a young girl who could see me and talk to me. I couldn't believe that she could be able to do this.

It happened again. I saw her again, the girl she spoke to me. I don't know who she is, but I can see her in my dreams at least.

I only dream when I am waiting for the sign. Waiting for whatever happens to happen. I see her there just in the distance. I hear her, but I am not sure what to do. I know she sees me, but…

Most of the time, that's where I wake up. Damn dream, why won't it ever go further? I want to know who she is and why she can talk to me. She doesn't even have the mark, so why can she talk to me?

As I stand waiting the hour of Mr. Kline's passing, I see her. Her ebony hair, curly and long. Half up in a braid, the other half free flowing as she walks down the road.

"Hey!" I screamed. She turns to me. She says something, I guess, but…

Damn time for work. Mr. Kline's passing has taken me from the dream. I take him to the transit station. To another call, this one Mrs. Eldrick, 97, and an anytime call. Means I have to sit beside her wherever she may be and wait.

Slowly, the machine beeps, and I find myself in a small village. I see the girl again.

A young girl, maybe ten years old. For a while, I watched her play. Then she asks if I want to play. I think I have just become her friend, as only she sees me. Her brother calls me imaginary because he can't see me. It doesn't bother me as long as she is here.

She offers me fake tea, but my cup is filled. I drink it, we talk, and when I ask her for her name….

Beeeeeeeepppp!!!!!! Flat line, play time over, daydream done. Mrs. Eldrick has let go.

Even though I dream more of her, I may never know who she is. I know she's just a dream, but I can't seem to get her out of my mind. I don't know what it is, but I keep thinking about her. The dream seemed to be at my moments when I am feeling down. I don't know why I have the dream then, but I do.

The more often the dream occurs, the closer to figuring out who the girl is. But these dreams always seem to wake up before I'm about to get to know her.

What can you do when you have no control over something, yet you wish it could be different? The only thing I can do is hope; the more dreams I have, the closer I get to her.

Chapter 4

The girl

She wasn't like the others. An outsider in her own world. No friends, no real friends that is to speak of. For a long time, she sat alone at lunch. Until the day she saw death.

At ten years of age, she saw him, Death, the Grimm Reaper, standing near Mr. Zann. Mr. Zann had been sick for a while. When she saw death, she gasped, waved at him, and smiled.

She could see that he, death, was a little confused. She just smiled and waved at him. The other kids teased and laughed at her because there was no one they could see she was waving at.

A few days later, she saw him again. Only this time, he, death, was standing outside her home. That was very unusual for her, but she needed to know why.

She snuck down the terrace and over to him. "Why are you here?" She asked. With a confused look at her, he answered, "Why can you see me when you have no mark?" "You mean it's not common?" She replied question. "No!" He answered.

Then, as quickly as death had appeared, he was gone. The time we actually spent more than a few hours together was when she found me. She came to my home and sat down, and waited for me, and by then she was about 16. Her parents threw her out and told her not to return to the village. She was no longer allowed there because she talked to death.

So, I guess in a way, it was my fault she was forced out of her house. When I got home, though I wasn't fully present, she just looked at me. I wasn't sure how she had found my home, but she had. She stared at me, but not in an angry way. Instead, she was happy to see me.

Inside my home, she could sense the death that surrounded me, and I was excited to discover someone would be there when I returned home from the jobs I had to do. I just hope that the years ahead are good.

Epilogue

You made it to the end.

Strange, isn't it? How a story about death isn't really about dying.

It's about remembering.

The mark comes for everyone, but maybe, just maybe, we're more than the ticking clock. Maybe we are the ones who see the unseen. Maybe we are the ones who linger, not out of fear — but out of hope.

She saw me.

And because of her, I saw myself.

So no, this isn't the end.

But it is a goodbye.

For now.

The end?